The Movie Novel

Little, Brown and Company
Hachette Book Group
1290 Avenue of the Americas, New York, NY 10104
Visit us at LBYR.com

First Edition: February 2019

Little, Brown and Company is a division of Hachette Book Group, Inc. The Little, Brown name and logo are trademarks of Hachette Book Group, Inc.

The publisher is not responsible for websites (or their content) that are not owned by the publisher.

Library of Congress Control Number 2018945945

ISBNs: 978-0-316-44476-7 (pbk.), 978-0-316-44478-1 (ebook)

Printed in the United States of America

LSC-C

10 9 8 7 6 5 4 3 2 1

The Movie Novel

Adapted by Sadie Chesterfield

Little, Brown and Company
New York   Boston

Chapter 1

June sat on the floor of her bedroom. She unrolled the giant piece of paper and began sketching the carousel. Her mom looked on, waiting to see what she'd draw next. At first June had thought she'd give the carousel a dozen horses with colorful saddles and reins, but now she wasn't so sure.

"*Hmmm…*" she whispered, her marker in her hand. "That sounds kinda 'been there, done that.' I think we can do better."

"You're right." Her mom smiled down at June. "I think Peanut *deserves* better."

They both turned to the row of dolls perched on June's dresser. There was Greta, the boar who was the leader of the group. She could run faster than any of the others. Then there was Steve, the porcupine who was in love with Greta. (June had made him out of an old pincushion.) June loved the two beavers, Gus and Cooper, who built everything in her imaginary amusement park, Wonderland. Boomer was the giant grizzly bear who welcomed visitors, but no one was as important as Peanut. Peanut the chimpanzee was the creator of Wonderland, the true genius, and June consulted him on everything she made.

"You come up with it, Mom!" June said, stumped.

"How could I not defer to the young visionary who came up with the Skyflinger?" Her mom smiled. The Skyflinger was one of the craziest rides in Wonderland. It rocketed passengers across the park using its super-fast robot arm.

"Don't make fun of me," June said, laughing. "I was only five when I made that!"

"I wasn't making fun of you, silly. I just...like it when the ideas come from you. Now, think....What kind of animal should Peanut put on your carousel?"

June glanced around her bedroom, her eyes lingering on her pet fish, Fred.

"Fish!" she called out.

"Just, like, any fish?"

"*Flying* fish!" June said. "And when you push the fin, the fish will come to life, and you can fly them all over the park!"

"Now we're talking, June!" Her mom picked the plush Peanut doll off the dresser. He was still one of June's favorite toys. June passed her mom the marker so she could put it in Peanut's hand.

"All you have to do is give Peanut his marker and whisper your wish into his ear…" her mom said, bringing her lips close to Peanut's ear. "Now, Peanut, here's what we want you to do: Take your marker and make us a carousel, but instead of horses, make flying fish…."

June could almost picture it, how Peanut would stand in front of the huge crowds in Wonderland, using his marker like a magic wand. It would spark with colorful electricity, and everyone would *ooohhh* and *aaaaah* as the most incredible carousel they'd ever seen appeared out of thin air.

"And when the fish fly through the concession stand, people will throw popcorn out in the air to feed them!" June cried, laughing again.

"So long as Boomer doesn't eat all the popcorn first." Her mom crumpled up the origami horse she was making and made an origami fish instead.

June nodded. Boomer was known for eating a lot...like really, really a lot.

Just then the door opened and June's dad peeked in. "Okay, June, time for bed." Then he looked at June's mom. "And you've got a DVR that's gonna run out of storage unless we start getting serious."

"Okay, Junebug...that's it for tonight." Her mom stood and helped June into bed. She tucked all the blankets in around her, just the way June liked, and kissed the top of her head. Then she set the origami fish right beside the bed.

"*Uhhh*...Mom?" June asked. "Do you ever feel like Wonderland is real? Or... maybe it could be?"

It was a fair question. June and her mom had spent hours thinking of all the tiny details of this imaginary place. Like the type of tea Steve drank every morning, or how Gus and Cooper liked to play pranks on the other mascots. They'd designed the Skyflinger and Happy Happy Land and decided that Peanut should have warm green eyes, not brown or blue or gold. Wouldn't it be cool if it really did exist somewhere?

June's mom thought about it for a beat. "Of course it could be...."

"Really?" June asked. "How do you know?"

"Because I know the girl who imagined it, and she can do anything."

"Good night, Junebug," her dad said, switching off the light.

But as soon as the door shut behind her parents, June went to work. She pulled her tablet from her nightstand and brought up more drawings of Wonderland. She'd been working on a design for a roller coaster, and she was starting to think it was time to make things a little more…well, *real*.

"Big day tomorrow!" she said, glancing at the row of mascots on her dresser. She hoped they were ready.

Chapter 2

As soon as June got up in the morning, she called her friend Banky from down the street. Banky was an Indian boy with huge brown eyes and a wild enthusiasm for just about everything. It seemed that whatever plan June dreamed up, Banky was always there to conspire with her.

June scanned the yard, which was filled with kids from the neighborhood. One team hammered together the roller coaster track, while another group dragged different supplies from June's parents' toolshed: hoses, nails, an old lawn mower, and scrap wood. They'd managed to put together June's roller coaster before her parents had even finished breakfast.

June put the final touches on the roller coaster car, which was just big enough for two people. She checked the screws on the tires and spray-painted a picture of Peanut on the side. She liked to put Peanut's picture on everything in Wonderland—cups, napkins, hats, bathroom stalls.

When June was sure the car was just right, she and Banky brought it up to the roof. "They said it couldn't be done," she called out to the crowd of kids gathered below. "But behold—the Grand Wonder!"

She stepped back, letting all the kids see the car perched at the top of the track. A few girls cheered. A boy cupped his hand over his mouth in disbelief. June and Banky climbed inside. She was in the front and he was right behind her.

"Who said it couldn't be done?" Banky whispered.

"They."

"Who's they?" Banky asked.

"It's just an expression. Don't bust me on a technicality." Then June turned back to the crowd, her voice booming. "Five hundred and sixty-two feet of track. An intergalactic spaceport complete with wormhole. And the *pièce de résistance*—that's French for 'super awesome'—a genuine loop-de-loop!"

"Uh…" Banky said uneasily as he stared over the roof ledge. "How high did you say the vertical drop is?"

"Forty-eight point eight feet!" June said. "That's fourteen point eight seven meters for the uninitiated."

She didn't feel scared at all. In fact, she was more excited than she'd ever been. One of her creations had finally come to life! She pulled down her goggles, getting ready for the big moment. "Commencing test run. All systems are a go. Five…four… three…two…one…"

"Can we talk about this?" whispered Banky.

But it was too late. Rodney, the boy in charge of launching them, pulled the fishing line, releasing the block underneath the coaster's front wheels. In an instant, the car was careening down the wooden track.

"*Aaaaaaaahhh!*" Banky screamed.

They flew through the air, finally catching on the bottom track. They whipped through the neighbor's yard, and Peaches, the neighbor's dog, started chasing them.

"Launching countermeasures!" June cried as she flung a piece of raw steak at him. The dog caught it in his mouth and started gnawing on it.

The car coasted along. Up ahead was the treadmill they'd set up to help with the coaster's speed. June liked to think of it as a turbo launcher, and as soon as they crossed over it, they were going three times faster. They sped into another neighbor's backyard and rounded a curb. They went through a few traffic cones, crossed the street, and spotted Moon Land up ahead. It was their friend's garage, and they'd decorated it to look as if they'd be coasting through space. Planets hung from the ceiling; twinkly stars sparkled against black curtains. There was only one problem: The garage door was closed.

"Open the spaceport!" June said.

Banky kept pressing the button on his remote, but it wasn't working.

"I'm trying! I'm trying!" he cried, and it finally began to open on the fourth try.

They were going full speed toward the

garage door as it slowly lifted up. There was no way it would open enough for them to get through. They were out of time!

"*Ahhh!* Duck!" June yelled.

They both sank down in their seats as far as they could. They slipped through the three-foot opening and then flew out the other side. June screamed in excitement. "Woo-hoo! Warp speed through a black hole! Now time for the grand finale... firing thrusters!"

June tugged on a string by the dash-board, and two fire extinguishers appeared on either side of the car. They exploded in a cloud of white smoke, blasting the roller coaster toward the loop-de-loop. But instead of going up and over the wooden track, the car broke right through it and careened toward an intersection.

"Brake! Brake!" June yelled, her heart beating fast. They didn't have much room for mistakes. They were heading toward the busy street!

Banky grabbed the brake lever and pulled as hard as he could, but it snapped right off. "It broke!" he screamed in panic. *"AAAAHHH!"*

The coaster raced forward. A huge truck swerved to avoid them. Drivers yelled and honked their horns, but June and Banky couldn't stop. They both squeezed their eyes shut, terrified of what would come next.

Chapter 3

June took a deep breath and then grabbed the steering wheel with both hands. Just before the coaster jumped the curb, she swerved right, keeping it on the sidewalk. They dodged the mailman and some people eating ice cream. Then she swerved again, avoiding a brick wall. But the car was going so fast she couldn't control it. Within seconds they were back on the street.

The car had a mind of its own. June could barely steer anymore. Instead, she yanked off the wheel. "Use this to pry off the thruster on the left!" she yelled, handing it to Banky as a station wagon sped past.

"Isn't that the steering wheel?" he asked.

"It was! Now, hurry!" June cried.

Banky leaned into the makeshift lever, jamming the rim of the wheel between the extinguisher and the car. He used all his weight to pry it free. As soon as it fell away, the car went into a screeching left turn, just narrowly avoiding a huge truck. But the force of the other extinguisher was so intense it blasted apart the car, sending June and Banky flying in opposite directions.

Banky went crashing through a neighbor's fence. The front seat of the car spun out the other way. It was a long while before it actually stopped. June sat up and felt her head and arms, making sure she wasn't hurt. She was a little dizzy, but, otherwise, she was okay.

"That was...awesome!" she yelled.

"I'm alive!" Banky observed cheerfully. "Thank Krishna!"

Within a few minutes, all the neighborhood kids had found them. Sara, a girl who lived two houses down, kept telling them how cool they were. Rodney, the boy who had pulled the fishing line, wanted to go next. June and Banky were so excited, they barely noticed the angry old man who was stomping toward them. A woman was walking down the sidewalk, her face as red as a beet.

"My garden!" she yelled.

"Someone's gonna pay!" the old man grumbled.

As if on cue, another piece of the man's fence fell down. June looked up, hoping Rodney or Sara or any of the other kids would say something, but the crowd had scattered in every direction. Only she and Banky were left, sitting in a pile of wood and metal pieces from the broken coaster.

"Uh-oh," June said. Her parents were not going to be happy about this.

Chapter 4

A gruff worker in an orange vest stomped up the front stairs and handed June's dad a bill. June's dad stared down at it. "That much for one fire hydrant?" he asked.

"My advice?" the worker said. "Military school. That's the kind of discipline your daughter needs."

June watched from her bedroom window as a few more neighbors joined the long line up her front walk. There was the woman whose garden they'd ruined, the man whose fence they'd broken, the neighbor who was angry about her dog getting loose, their mailman, and then three other neighbors who June had never seen before. At this rate, her parents would be fielding complaints until midnight.

She slunk down against the wall, wondering how long she'd be grounded. After hearing the fifth conversation, she thought she'd be lucky if her parents let her out for senior prom. She was thinking of what to say, when her mom peeked around the door.

"The thing about military school…" June started. "It's usually far away. Think about how much you'd miss me. Who would really be the one getting punished?"

"We're not sending you to military school." Her mom sighed.

"You're not?" June actually grinned.

"Oh no," her mom said. "Because military school doesn't have nearly the amount of chores you're going to be subjected to."

"I guess I walked right into that one…."

"What were you thinking, June?" Her mom furrowed her brows. "Do you know how lucky you are? It could have been a whole lot worse than a raspberry on your elbow."

"I was just listening to you," June tried. "You said Wonderland could be real. And that I could do anything."

"I never want you to stop using your imagination, Junebug," her mom said. "But I need you to also remember to be practical and safe. I can't imagine what I'd do if something happened to you."

June took a deep breath, letting it sink in. She knew her mom was right. It wasn't the safest or most practical idea to build a super-duper roller coaster that tore through the entire neighborhood, and she could've really hurt herself. Or Banky. But she still was just the tiniest bit proud.

"Even though I shouldn't have done it," she said, "did you think what I built was cool?"

"It doesn't matter what I think," her mom said. But then she glanced sideways at the dolls scattered across June's floor. "But Gus and Cooper, on the other hand, would have been crazy impressed."

"Yeah." June laughed a little. "But Steve would've had a heart attack, huh?"

Steve was a porcupine, but sometimes June was convinced he was part chicken. He was afraid of everything!

"Yes!" June's mom laughed, too.

"So…we can keep building more of Wonderland?" June said, a little nervous to hear the answer.

"Of course," her mom said. "But, June, without wrecking the neighborhood."

"Right." June agreed. "Without wrecking the neighborhood…"

And that was how it began. After June finished about a hundred billion trillion chores, and her parents had made peace with every single one of the neighbors, she and her mom started building the largest, most expansive version of Wonderland yet. They drew a huge blueprint and came up with even more ideas for spectacular rides. It wasn't long before every wall in June's room was covered with new designs.

Using some gears they'd found in an old grandfather clock, June and her mom built a scale model called Clockwork Swings. It spun around and around, sending the tiny swings flying in a circle. June considered it the heart of the park, and when it was turned on, the whole place came to life. They built a statue of Peanut for the front entrance and a gift shop where everyone could buy the different Peanut dolls. They even made gates and lakes and tiny trees so the model would look as real as possible.

Then, one night when June and her parents were watching a movie about an astronaut, June was inspired to make a zero-gravity ride in which guests could float in space. She and her mom ran upstairs and gave Peanut the marker, and her mom whispered in his ear the way she did every time they wanted to create a new ride. Together they built a beautiful starry sky visitors could float through. It was one of the most magical places June had ever dreamed up.

After that ride, the ideas poured out of her. It wasn't long before the tiny models spread out over June's dresser and night-stand and then over the rug in the middle of her floor. But she kept creating anyway, so Wonderland grew even bigger. Soon the miniature rides and signs were all over the living room and dining room, too. Kids in the neighborhood stopped by every afternoon to see the latest models June had built.

June was so happy building Wonderland she didn't really notice at first when her mom started to feel sick. She told herself everything would be fine, and that as long as her mom smiled when she saw June's newest model ride, there really was nothing to worry about. *Yes,* she thought one night, when she heard her parents whispering behind their bedroom door. *It's nothing. Everything will be okay.*

When her parents got a call from the doctor one afternoon, June did not believe the news. It was only when she saw her mother's face, and the tears pooling in her eyes, that she got scared.

Chapter 5

June kept working on Wonderland, even when her mom couldn't build it with her anymore. She was creating a huge slide with different twists and turns in it. She had used a whole box of bendy straws, taping them all together, trying to see how high it could go. When she finally got to a stopping point, she knocked on her mom's bedroom door.

"Bendy Straw Slide is almost done," she said, holding it in the air.

Her mom was lying in bed. Her dad was with her.

"Look at you...." Her mom offered her a small smile as she sat up in bed. "Come here, baby girl. I want to talk to you for a minute."

June sat next to her mom and leaned on her shoulder. She stared up at her mom with big, hopeful eyes, wondering if this was it. Maybe this was the good news they'd all wished for. Maybe her mom was getting better.

"You know Mommy's sick. There are some special doctors who might be able to help me," she said. "But I may have to go away for a while to see them."

"How long are you going away?" June asked, her voice cracking.

"That just depends," her mom said. "But believe me, I am going to do everything I can to try and get better. Model patient."

"We'll go visit, honey...." Her dad put his hand on June's arm.

June could feel a lump in the back of her throat. What was she going to do without her mom? She needed her. To build Wonderland and to make jokes and to just…be her mom. This wasn't fair.

"Hey, I know this is scary," her mom said, "but you keep that little light in you shining bright."

"I don't know if I can…." As soon as she said it, June knew it was true. How was she supposed to go on pretending as if everything were normal? As if she were happy?

Tears slipped down her cheeks. She didn't want her mom to leave. Not now, not ever.

"Well, I do," her mom said. "Because you are the wonder in Wonderland."

Her mom leaned in, brushing her nose against June's. Her dad kept his hand on June's shoulder, trying to comfort her, but she felt as if her whole world were falling apart.

Her mother went to the hospital the following week. June watched her drive away. She tried to be brave and strong, but the house felt so much emptier without her mom in it. Even worse, June started worrying about her dad. What if something happened to him?

She sat in her bedroom, staring at the blueprint she and her mom had made together. They'd drawn a picture of themselves and written their names inside a heart in the corner. It didn't feel right working on Wonderland now that her mom was away. Her dad kept coming up with ideas for it, but it wasn't the same. And when June talked to her mom on the phone, her voice sounded strange and far off. How could June tell her about all her different dreams and creations when her mom was so sick?

Keep that little light in you shining bright, June thought, remembering her mother's words.

But as she looked at Clockwork Swings and the Skyflinger and all the other things they'd built together, she couldn't bring herself to keep creating. It just made her miss her mom more.

So she went through the house, packing up all the tiny models in a cardboard box. She plucked the mascots off her dresser one by one and put them on top. Peanut was last, and as she closed the lid, she felt an immediate sense of relief.

Maybe it was better not to think of all the good times they'd shared.

Maybe it was better to forget.

Chapter 6

If only June's friends could forget, too...

Her mom had been gone a few weeks when Banky showed up at her door, holding a giant box. A bunch of neighborhood kids were behind him, and he was smiling his biggest we-came-to-cheer-you-up smile.

It wasn't working.

"Hey, June!" he said. "My parents got me this drone kit, and we could really use your help putting it together. Thought we could use it for Wonderland."

June could feel her dad watching her from the living room.

"Go on, June," he called out. "That'll be fun."

"*Uhhhh…*" June stalled. "Is that FAA certified for use in a residential area? Those things can be insanely hazardous."

"Well, we're insanely bored," Banky said. "And, dare I say, desperate. We've stooped to repeatedly rolling each other down a hill for fun, and I don't think Raj can handle it anymore."

Behind him, his little brother walked around in circles dizzily.

"It was great seeing you, Banky, but maybe tomorrow," June said as she closed the door on her friend.

June tried to walk past her dad into the kitchen, but he was staring at her intently. "Junie," he started, "can we talk about what's going on with you?"

"All they want to do is play Wonderland," June said, crossing her arms over her chest.

"Well, you know—"

"Don't make this a thing," she said. "It's not a thing. It's just—"

Before she could finish her thought, the doorbell rang again. She yanked the door open, expecting to see Banky still standing there, but, instead, it was her aunt Albertine and her uncle Tony. They both had loud voices and big, baritone laughs.

"Surprise!" they yelled in unison.

"Heard you wanted to see your favorite aunt and uncle," Aunt Albertine started, "but they sent us instead."

"HEY-O!" Uncle Tony chuckled. "That's why I married her. Now, bring it in for the good stuff, kiddo."

Both Uncle Tony and Aunt Albertine embraced her in one of their bone-crushing hugs. June could barely breathe. Then they smushed her cheeks together, which was one of their signature moves.

"It's good to see you," June said, talking

through the squish. "Even though you always do this to my cheeks."

June's dad dragged a few giant suitcases in from the porch. "Jeez!" he said, laughing. "What did you pack—the whole house? I thought you guys were only coming for two nights."

"Yes, well, it's just the essentials," Aunt Albertine said. "And, anyway, we bought a luggage set and we wanted to use all the bags."

"Oh!" Uncle Tony shouted suddenly. "Get the present!"

"Right!" Aunt Albertine said, searching through her bag. She pulled out a box with a Ferris wheel on the front. "We have a present for you, June! It's a Ferris wheel! I thought it would be just perfect for your whole Wonderland model."

June stared down at the box in her aunt's hand. "Oh…uh…"

Aunt Albertine glanced around the

living room, noticing that the floor and dining room table weren't covered with miniatures anymore. A fire was going in the fireplace, and all the rides that had been lined up on the mantle had disappeared. She looked thoroughly confused.

"Where'd that all go?" she asked.

"We...we put Wonderland away," June's dad answered.

"That's a shame," Aunt Albertine said. "I told your mom just yesterday that we'd help you build it."

"What do you say?" Uncle Tony cried. "Let's rebuild Wonderland!"

Before June could say another word, Aunt Albertine started digging through the hall closet, where she'd put her coat. She dragged out a few boxes that contained the Wonderland models from the living room.

"Hey, hey," June's dad tried. "Why don't we talk about something else? Weather? Tax returns? Literally anything else?"

But Aunt Albertine and Uncle Tony could not be stopped. June's aunt grabbed the blueprint off the top of the box and unfolded it, revealing the picture of the park and all its attractions: the Skyflinger and Zero G Land and the row of trees her mom had planted by the north gate. June could feel the lump rising in the back of her throat. She didn't need to talk about her mom or Wonderland. She didn't want to see any of this.

"It's the blueprint for Wonderland," Aunt Albertine said, as if it weren't obvious already.

"I don't play with that anymore." There was an edge to June's words. "Please—put that away."

"But this is a beautiful thing you and your mom did together, darling," Aunt Albertine went on, softening her voice more than she ever had before. "To create something so real! You can remem—"

"Wonderland isn't real!" June snapped, unable to stand it anymore. "It never could be real! And even if it was, it's the last place in the world I'd wanna visit!"

June snatched the blueprint from Aunt Albertine, ran to the fireplace, and tossed it onto the logs. She watched as the flames engulfed it. One side curled up and turned black, breaking into ash as the fire spread over it.

"Oh no!" Aunt Albertine ran to her, horrified at what had happened. "Oh, Junie!"

June watched as the fire consumed the rest of the blueprint. Just before the last piece burned, she spotted the drawing she and her mother had made of themselves. They'd signed the top of it and made a heart around their picture.

Without thinking, June reached into the flames and tried to grab that piece before it was destroyed, but her father ran to her and held her back. She struggled and broke free of him, darting toward the stairs. Tears welled in her eyes. She knew her aunt and uncle meant well; she knew Banky meant well, too. But she couldn't deal with all those good intentions anymore.

Why couldn't everyone just let her be?

"I'm sorry," June muttered as she ran up the stairs. She didn't stop until she got to her room. Then she threw herself down on her bed and broke into sobs.

Chapter 7

June spent the next few days busying herself with household chores. She'd never realized how much time school took up. Now that it was summer, and she was home all day, it was much harder to distract herself. She'd already read a hundred books and played on the computer and organized the refrigerator and medicine cabinet and every closet in the house. She was vacuuming the rug in the living room when her dad came in.

"Great news!" he said as the vacuum stopped. "Tomorrow is math camp! And

I know it's important to clean an already-clean house, but why don't you channel some of this nervous energy into packing?"

June folded the blanket on the couch. Then she noticed something horrible. One of her dad's golf balls was on the floor.

"This is dangerous!" she said, picking it up. "And I'm not going to math camp. They're just going to give me sad eyes. Besides, I have a lot to do around here!"

She sat down at the computer. "Is that a three-month or six-month renewal on your wheatgrass deliveries?" she asked, pulling up a spreadsheet of different things to do around the house. "I'll put in six."

"June, all I'm saying is—"

"Your triglycerides are still on the high end," she went on, ignoring him. "I'm not taking any chances with your health."

"June..." her dad tried. "You can't stay in here forever...."

"I just know I need to be home this summer to take care of you."

"June, today I got dressed and I made breakfast all by myself," he said. "As I have been doing for the last forty-one years. The first seven, I needed a little help, but since then I've been okay."

Just then the toaster started smoking. Her dad had set the dial too high, and now the toast was burning. The smoke alarm started wailing. June was sure it was a sign.

"I'm not going to math camp," she said firmly, looking her dad directly in the eye. He needed her here, at home. Maybe even more than he realized.

But June *was* going to math camp. No matter how much she refused, her dad wouldn't budge. The next morning they met the bus in the mall parking lot. Dozens of kids were saying good-bye to their parents.

"Don't put the avocados next to the bananas," June warned, trying to remember all the little mistakes her dad might make. "They ripen too fast. And please leave the toaster set to three—you know you don't like it when the edges are too crispy."

"My morning toast will be fine," her dad said.

"Oh, and the milk in the fridge...it could be out of date so make sure you check it—"

"Junie, Junie," he said, "I'm going to be okay. I know this is a big step. Mom and I are both so proud of you for going. We'll both call you, and as soon as you come home, we'll go visit her together. Now, get out there on the Abacus Obstacle Course and skin a knee!"

"Okay."

"Promise?" her dad said, hugging her.

"Promise."

June knew there was no point in arguing anymore. Her dad kissed her on the head, and she walked to the bus with the others. When she got on, a dozen strangers stared back at her. Her stomach twisted in knots.

"Hey, June Bailey, saved you a seat!" a familiar voice called out. Banky was sitting toward the back of the bus. He slid over to make room for her. "This is going to be the best summer ever!"

June sat next to him, relieved to have a friend. Banky's whole family had come to the bus to see him off. They'd even made signs with his name on them.

"Hey, campers!" Shannon, the senior counselor, said as the bus pulled onto the street. "Everybody here is heading to Camp Awe+Sum, right? If you're not, you're on the"—she made a diamond shape with her fingers—"rhom-bus."

Everyone laughed. Banky turned to June and smiled. "I love geometry humor."

June watched her dad as the bus pulled away. He grew smaller and smaller in the distance. She still worried he'd slip and fall or get sick or hurt himself in some silly way, but when the bus erupted into song, it was kind of hard not to join in.

"Oh my!" they all sang. *"Here comes pi! Three point one four one five. A constant we all know, the famous* ratiooooooooo."

As the song went on, June sang louder, joining Banky. She was surprised it felt so good. *"Oh my! Here comes pi! How many can you memorize? It goes on and on, a never-ending song...."*

She pulled her lunch bag onto her lap and grabbed a juice box from it. It was only then that she noticed the note tucked inside. Her dad had packed all her favorite snacks and written a message on a napkin.

June, have a great summer! I love you! Miss you, Dad.

It was supposed to make her feel better, but she just kept staring at her dad's words. *Miss you.* He was going to miss her—of course he would. What would he do with all his time? What if he slipped and fell on something? Who would call the ambulance? Who would get him soup if he got sick?

"This is a terrible mistake," June said to herself as the song grew louder around her. She suddenly felt panicky. "What was I thinking? I can't leave him alone for the entire summer...."

Banky was still singing along beside her. *"Well, why is the obtuse triangle—"*

"Banky, I need your help," June said, turning to him. "I need to get home."

"What?" Banky said. "Your dad will flip. We're talking eternal groundation."

"But he knows he can't function without me." She pointed to the note. "Look at this. 'Miss you.' It's like a cry for help."

"Uh…I don't know, June." Banky stared at the note. "I think you might be reading a bit too much into this."

"I'll take the hiking trails through the forest, and I'll be there before lunch," June said, looking out the window. They were barely even a mile away from the mall. "It's a no-brainer. But first, I need to get off the bus. And you have to help me—please?"

"Ugh…" Banky looked nervous. "Okay."

"Yes! Banky, I could kiss you!" June cried.

"Really?" Banky said, his eyes wide.

"*Ewwwww,*" June said. The thought of kissing boys was so unappealing. "No."

"Right," Banky said, disappointed.

"Now, what can I use…?"

June pulled a bunch of snacks from her lunch bag. She mushed up some of the chips and fruit gummies in her hand and then put the mixture into her water bottle. With a few shakes, it looked perfect. She whispered a few quick instructions to Banky, and then he stood up in the aisle.

"I don't think I'm feeling very well at this moment," he called out to the counselor. "I think I might…"

He sat back down and grabbed the water bottle from June. "Oh, I can't hold it in anymore! Oh no! It's here, it's here!" Then he dumped what was in the bottle onto the floor. *"Bleerrrrrrrghhhh!"*

"Barf!" a camper yelled.

"Ewwww!" another kid screamed. "Stop the bus!"

The bus screeched to a halt. All the kids ran out, Banky right behind them. June sank down in her seat, waiting until she was sure she was the last one left. Then, when Shannon and the bus driver rounded up the kids on the side of the road, she slipped off and headed for the forest.

She turned back one last time. Banky was watching her go. She brought her hand to her mouth and blew him a kiss, and it looked as if Banky fainted, his eyes fluttering back in his head. Then June started through the forest, trying to find where the hiking trails picked up.

Chapter
8

June could still hear the campers singing as she made her way up the hill. They were back on the bus and driving away without ever realizing she was gone. She hiked a few more yards and found the path she'd been on a dozen times before with her parents. It couldn't have been more than a half-hour walk back to town.

A breeze whipped through the trees, sending leaves flying with it. She turned onto the path and saw the strangest sight... a piece of paper drifting in front of her. The edges were black and burnt. As she reached for it, she recognized the drawing. It was part of the blueprint she'd made with her mom. Even as it turned in the wind, she could see their picture surrounded by a heart.

"Wait…why is this here?" June asked herself as she chased after it. It seemed impossible. Had it been blown up the chimney? How did it make it outside?

She reached for it again, but the wind picked up, and the paper flew just out of her grasp. It danced around her as if it were alive and then smacked her playfully on the nose. She rubbed her eyes, certain she was dreaming, but then the piece fluttered away.

June ran after it, darting through the forest. She jumped rocks and shrubs and passed over a small stream, until she was surrounded on all sides by towering trees. She ran faster, picking up speed, but her foot caught on a broken branch, and she stumbled forward. She fell on the ground, and the piece of paper landed right in her hand.

"Gotcha!" She laughed, holding it up.

She stood and turned around, realizing she'd completely lost the trail. She didn't even know which direction she'd come from. She stared down at the dirt, noticing a piece of metal glinting under the leaves. Something about it seemed familiar....

Tucking the piece of paper safely in her pocket, she went to the strange object and pulled back a big section of vines. It was a roller coaster car—*her* roller coaster car. There was even a picture of Peanut on the side. *What is going on?!* she thought. *This can't be real. This isn't really happening.*

But when she dusted off the car, she could see it was on some kind of track. She climbed inside and pulled the safety bar down over her lap, just as she would on a real roller coaster. Almost as soon as the bar clicked into place, she tried to pull it back up, but it wouldn't budge.

The wheels creaked. She could feel the coaster rolling forward, inch by inch, toward the edge of the hill. It started picking up speed, and she had to hold her hand to her face so she wouldn't get hit by stray branches. The car swooped down over the grassy track, then up to a high vista. When she looked around, she couldn't believe her eyes.

In a canyon far below was a sprawling amusement park. It looked as if it hadn't been touched in years. The trees and bushes were overgrown, and all the rides looked as if they'd stopped working decades before.

"Is this...?" June muttered, unable to even form the words. *It can't be...*

Almost as soon as she thought it, the car hit a vertical drop, and her stomach leaped. She felt that weightless feeling she had when she and Banky were on their coaster, and she clung tightly to the safety bar, trying to stay tucked in. The car raced around the track, up and over and side to side.

"*Whoaaaa!*" June screamed. "*WHOA!*"

A wheel broke off, and the car struggled to stay on the track. June was jerked right and left as she clung to the bar, holding on for dear life. Just when she was sure the coaster was coming apart, the car crested one last hill and came to a stop. The safety bar popped up and June climbed out. But she was dizzy from the ride, and she slipped, plummeting off the track and into the trees below.

Chapter 9

June landed on the ground with a thud. She stood up slowly, brushing herself off, and tried to see if she were hurt. There were leaves and twigs in her hair, and her knees were sore from the fall, but otherwise she was okay. She glanced around, realizing she was in the middle of the park.

"No way," she said, staring out at the rusted rides with a huge smile on her face. All her creations were there. She could see the Skyflinger peeking out above the others. "How is this possible? Hello?"

Just then she spotted something familiar.

She ran over to the gold statue that stood at the front of the park. It was covered with vines and ivy, but it was him. It was really him.

"Peanut…" she said, bringing her hand to her mouth. The gold statue of the chimpanzee towered above her. "I'm in Wonderland."

She glanced up the hill, noticing the dark clouds that loomed in the distance. It looked as if a storm were coming, which was strange. Wonderland was the one place where it never rained. She'd imagined the sun as always shining brightly in the sky. It was always supposed to have perfect weather.

Off in the distance, she noticed a small blue speck on the horizon. It was moving. It grew bigger and bigger, until she could just make out a giant bear. He was running right at her.

"Boomer the Welcome Bear is here, too?" June laughed. He was huge, with fuzzy blue fur and a brown muzzle.

But as Boomer got closer, June noticed he wasn't smiling. He looked completely panicked, and behind him, the rest of the mascots were running, too. He darted right past her.

"Run for your life!" he screamed.

June stood frozen in place, confused. Why was Boomer charging out of the park? Why were the other mascots following him? Were they playing some sort of game? Were they pretending?

"Hey!" June called, trying to get the mascots' attention. Greta the boar, Steve the porcupine, and the two beavers, Gus and Cooper, were all racing past. They barely even looked at her.

"Get moving, pip-squeak!" Greta yelled as she went by. She was short with brown fur, and she had tiny white tusks sticking out of either side of her mouth. Her hairy black tail swished behind her.

"What's going on?" June tried to catch up, but they were all moving so fast. "Why are we chasing Boomer?"

"We're not chasing him," Gus said, out of breath. He was taller than Cooper, with reddish fur and a chip in his front tooth. "They're chasing us."

He glanced over his shoulder as he ran. June turned back, noticing the giant dust cloud for the first time. It looked as if something were coming after them, but she couldn't tell what.

"Regroup at Rocket Road!" Greta yelled to the others. "We need to funnel that army into that rocket."

Army? June thought as she sprinted as fast as she could. *What army?*

They caught up with Boomer at the enormous, rusted Confetti Ship, which June had created the year before. But now it was real—a huge multistory spaceship that towered over them. A large hose connected the bottom of the ship to a water pump. When the pressure built up enough, it was supposed to launch the rocket over the park.

"Gus, gnaw that awning down!" Greta said, pointing to a pergola over the entrance. "Cooper, start the pump! And, Steve—"

"I'll draft up an exit plan," Steve said, nodding. His gray quills stuck up in every direction. June could barely see his eyes behind his giant, bulbous pink nose.

"You're the bait," Greta explained.

Steve let out a deep sigh. "Of course I am."

June hid behind the antigravity ball pit with Greta and Boomer. They watched as Steve ran out front toward the giant swarming dust cloud. As it came closer, June could see it was actually a pack of

Wonder Chimp souvenir dolls. June and her mom had created them years ago for the gift shop as tiny tributes to the park's creator. The little plush monkeys were each dressed in a different costume. There was a bee, an astronaut, a frog, a rabbit, a pirate, and more. But now they didn't seem like cute, harmless dolls. They seemed scary—*wild.*

"Every day is a wonderful day, is a wonderful day, in Wonderland!" they sang in unison.

"Boomer," Greta whispered. "You protect her with your life."

Then she ran off, disappearing behind another ride.

"What is going on around here?" June whispered to the giant bear. He was twice as tall as her dad.

"What does it look like?" Boomer said, pulling June back so the Chimpanzombies wouldn't see her. "We're at war."

"War?" That was the silliest thing she'd ever heard. She had created this place, and everyone was supposed to be happy here. No one ever yelled or cried or was scared. "There's no fighting in Wonderland," she said.

"Stay put. Because if they see us, they will..." Boomer's eyelids started to fall shut. He suddenly looked very, very tired. "Uh-oh—save yourself!"

Before he could say another word, he collapsed on the ground. Now he was lying there, snoring peacefully, as if they weren't in danger at all. The poor bear looked as if he were suffering from some kind of late-onset hibernation disorder.

"They'll what?" June nudged Boomer in the side. "Finish the sentence! They'll what?"

But Boomer kept snoring. June peeked out from behind the ball pit. The tiny monkeys were banging on everything. They moved in a pack, destroying everything in front of them. They'd reduced a whole building to dust when Steve popped out from a hatch underneath the Confetti Ship.

"Hey, guys! Over here!" he yelled to the Chimpanzombies. "Dinner is served!"

All the Chimpanzombies turned their heads at once. They eyed Steve for a second. Then they took off toward the Confetti Ship. Steve disappeared inside the hatch, leaving it open so they could follow him in. June watched, her heart pounding in her chest. She'd never been so terrified.

"I'm outta here," she said when the last Chimpanzombie darted toward the ship. She sprinted as fast as she could toward the carousel at the other end of the park. She glanced over her shoulder as she ran, noticing that Steve had climbed out of the top of the rocket and locked the Wonder Chimp dolls inside. Greta counted off, and then the Confetti Ship launched into the air. Within seconds it exploded. Stuffing and fabric and different Chimpanzombie body parts rained from the sky.

June didn't stop until she reached the carousel. She slung her backpack over her shoulder while trying to process the rocket and the dolls and the giant explosion in the sky. She listened to the park, which was now quiet, and tried to calm herself down.

"This isn't really happening," she said to herself. "I'm…I'm having a fever dream."

"Check it out!" a voice said somewhere behind her. "A backpack!"

"Could be treats!"

She felt someone tug the bag away from her. She turned to see the two beavers, Gus and Cooper, running away. "That's mine!" she yelled after them. "Give it back!"

But they didn't stop until they were several yards away. They rummaged through the backpack as if June weren't right there, watching them. They pulled out different snacks, holding them up and hooting and hollering as if they'd just won the lottery. They were so revved up they started wrestling each other, tumbling around on the ground.

June stepped behind a tree, a little nervous. She'd created Gus and Cooper, and she'd made them mischievous pranksters, but she wasn't so sure she wanted to hang out with them in real life. If this even *was* real life.

"Let's have a little lookie-loo!" Steve called, running over to Gus and Cooper. He grabbed the backpack. "With a self-reminder that this is an utter invasion of another's privacy—"

"Hold the roll, cutie pie!" Greta pushed past Steve and stuck her nose in June's bag.

Gus, Cooper, Steve, and Greta were surrounding it when Boomer appeared on the other side of the carousel. At some point he must've woken up, and now he looked completely panicked, his brown eyes wide.

"The Chimpanzombies!" he said breathlessly. "They got her, didn't they? It's all my doing! All thanks to my late-onset hibernation disorder!"

He suddenly passed out again, slamming into Greta on his way to the ground.

"*Ow!*" Greta yelled.

"Go to your happy place…" Boomer muttered in his sleep.

June stared at the mascots' panicked faces. The beavers were still rolling around on the ground, arguing, but Greta and Steve looked as if they might cry. June stepped out from where she was hiding and walked toward them, a little uncertain.

"It's okay," she said. "They didn't get me."

She thought they'd be relieved, but the beavers just kept fighting, and Greta and

Steve looked confused. There was no fanfare or happy greeting. June just stood there, waiting for them to say something.

Steve picked up some of the quills he'd lost. Greta was scowling, as if she'd gotten a whiff of something terrible. Gus and Cooper nearly knocked over June as they charged at each other, and Boomer was fast asleep.

What had happened to the joyful mascots? Boomer never used to fall asleep before, and Gus and Cooper would never fight. What had happened to all the laughs and fun they'd shared?

June Bailey loves to create things. Her imagination runs totally wild!

Her favorite project is a big amusement park called Wonderland. She's designing it with her mom.

Trying to escape a trip to math camp,
June wanders into a nearby forest.

Deep in the woods, she finds a mysterious
abandoned roller coaster car. When she
gets in, it starts to move...

...bringing her to Wonderland! The amusement park she'd worked so hard on with her mom has come to life! But how? June sets out to explore.

Suddenly, a giant blue bear races by.
It's Boomer the Welcome Bear!

June recognizes the other characters
from her imaginary amusement park.

Greta the boar is in charge of park security. She's fearless!

Steve the porcupine is in charge of safety. He has a bit of a crush on Greta, but he has trouble telling her about it.

Gus and Cooper are the beavers in charge of construction and engineering.

Peanut is the leader of the park. His magical marker lets him create the attractions in the park.

But the park is not quite how June remembers it. It has fallen into disrepair. June and the gang will have to explore the entire magical area...

...and put their heads together to come up with a plan that will restore Wonderland to its former glory!

June is very glad she met all these new friends. She's determined to help them save the park.

June Bailey is going on the adventure of her life in Wonderland!

Chapter 10

You're so..." June said, searching for the right word.

"Pathetic," Greta jumped in.

"I didn't say that!" June tried.

"You didn't have to." Greta frowned. She looked June up and down as she approached her, studying her fox sweatshirt and the shaggy red bob that always fell in her eyes. "So, you got a name, Haircut?"

"I'm June."

"Hello, June," Steve said. "My name is—"

"Steve," June replied. "I know who you are."

Gus looked genuinely excited. "You know who we are?"

"I didn't think anyone still remembered..." Cooper said a little sadly.

"You guys are the *wonder* in Wonderland," June said. "Or at least you were... What happened to this place?"

Boomer sat up and rubbed his eyes. He'd just caught the last bit of the conversation, and now he was staring at June, his face serious. "The Darkness happened...." He nodded to the dark cloud hanging over the other side of the park. "It came when Clockwork Swings began to slow. And brought with it—"

"All right, bring it down," Greta said, making fun of his serious tone.

"Okay, here we go," Boomer tried again. "It was a day just like any other here in

Wonderland...when the strangest thing happened: Clockwork Swings, the heart of the park, came to a dead stop. And that's when we first saw it: the Darkness. It brought an evil that transformed the Wonder Chimp dolls into an army of Chimpanzombies. Every day since, the chimps have waged war, tearing apart the park and feeding it piece by piece into the Darkness...never to be seen again."

June glanced around at the park. Many of the rides had giant sections missing from them. There was wreckage piled along the main path. "There was nothing you could do? Not even Peanut?" she asked. Then she realized that he was missing. "Where is Peanut?"

"He ventured out on his own to try and restart Clockwork Swings by hand," Boomer explained.

"Why didn't he use his magic?" June asked.

"He just said that he knew restarting Clockwork Swings was the only way to bring the life back into Wonderland. But..." Boomer trailed off, unable to go on.

June had to put the pieces of the story together herself. As Peanut crossed the bridge to the far side of the park, he was swarmed by the Chimpanzombies. He hadn't been seen since.

"We lost any hope of turning Clockwork Swings back on and one day restoring the park to all its former glory," Steve said sadly.

"Clockwork Swings..." June whispered to herself. She pulled the piece of blueprint from her pocket and studied it. It had the picture of her and her mom on it, but it also had part of the blueprint for Clockwork Swings. The design showed how all the pieces worked.

"Hey! Whatcha got?" Gus asked. He yanked the paper out of her hands. "It's a blueprint...of the park?"

"Seems like Little Miss Muffet graffitied her name on it," Cooper said as June grabbed the paper back. He was short and yellowish brown, with whiskers that curled at the ends.

"It's not graffiti," she said.

Greta looked confused. "How do you have a blueprint of Wonderland?"

"Umm..." June tried to think of the best way to say it. "My mom and I invented Wonderland when I was little, and somehow it came to life."

Greta snorted in disbelief. "That's gotta be the most—"

"Splendiferous news ever!" Boomer yelled.

"Why don't you just go back to sleep, Boomer?" Greta asked.

"I believe it in her eyes," Boomer said.

"Because if she really is the creator of Wonderland, she can fix Clockwork Swings."

"Well..." June muttered. She didn't really know how to fix Clockwork Swings. At least not yet. She had the blueprint and she could try, but what about the Darkness? And the Chimpanzombies? Would fixing Clockwork Swings really fix all that?

"Well, that is *not* where I thought this discourse was heading," Steve said, but he was staring off in the distance, somewhere behind June. "I was imagining that you were a—honey...honey bee!"

"Huh?" June asked. "I'm not a honey bee."

Steve could barely speak. Suddenly, his eyes were huge, and he was frozen in place. "Ra-ra-ra-rabbit!"

"Steve," Greta whispered to him. "You're embarrassing the team."

"Death!" Steve yelled out of nowhere.

A bewildered June stared at Steve, trying

to understand. Why had he suddenly lost the ability to speak? What was wrong with him? Was this some new ride he was talking about?

"I am so confused right now about what a 'death rabbit' is," June said.

But then she heard the chanting. It was far off, the words just barely audible over the wind. *"Splen-diddy-doo! Splen-diddy-doo!"* The Skyflinger had come to life, controlled by a few of the Chimpanzombies they hadn't caught in the Confetti Ship. The giant robot arm picked up a metal sphere and approached June and the mascots. It loomed over them, ready to strike.

"Boomer, go secure the safe house!" Greta said, springing into action. "Guys, scatter!"

They all ran in different directions. The Skyflinger launched the sphere, smashing it down where they had been standing just moments before. June sprinted for cover, still holding the blueprint in her hand. The honey bee doll and the rabbit doll she'd made for the gift shop were now in the Skyflinger.

She didn't have much time....

Chapter 11

Gus and Cooper ran into one of the Skyflinger spheres for cover, but then they got trapped inside. Steve hopped onto June's back. He was too scared to move, so June carried him all the way to the fish carousel and hid behind one of the fish-drawn chariots.

"We gotta get out of here," June said, watching as the Skyflinger launched Greta through the air. The boar landed in one of the swing seats, and she was so round she got stuck. "Think, June, think, think, think, think...."

Steve stared off at the concession stand. "We go in five...."

June frowned. "That could never work."

What was Steve thinking? They couldn't just run to the concession stand. Honey Bee and Rabbit would see them.

"Right, we skip," Steve corrected. "Skip like there's no tomorrow!"

Without finishing his thought, Steve took off toward the concession stand. As soon as the Chimpanzombie looked at him, he lost half his quills from fright. He scrambled away, but the Skyflinger chucked a metal sphere at him, catching him inside.

"*Tra-la-la-la!* Ow! Ow!" he said as the ball rolled through a vat of chocolate fondue near the snack bar.

With four of the mascots captured, June knew she was their only hope. She jumped onto the carousel fish and took a deep breath. "Please work, please work....

When you push the fin…" she said to herself, pressing down as hard as she could on the fish's fin. "The fish will come to life!"

The fish started spinning in circles. June's head whipped around, and she screamed. Then the fish took flight, soaring into the air. But June couldn't get control of it. It did another pirouette, then another, as she tried to steer the wild fish.

"Would you like to go to Fireworks Falls?" the fish said finally, as if it were her tour guide.

"No! Take me to Happy Happy Land!" June yelled.

"Detouring to Happy Happy Land," the fish said politely.

June pulled at the reins, trying to hold on, but the Skyflinger was right behind her. It stomped along, crushing rides and games in Toddler's Paradise. When they got to Happy Happy Land, cheerful music filled the air. Then the Skyflinger crushed the ride with its giant foot, reducing it to rubble, and everything went silent again.

"Would you like to stop for an ice cream?" the fish asked.

"No, no! Exit, exit, exit!" June cried. The Skyflinger chucked the metal sphere Gus and Cooper were in. It went rolling past her and disappeared from sight. She could still hear the two beavers screaming inside it.

Within minutes, June could see the exit up ahead. Her heart leaped. She'd figure out what went wrong in Wonderland later. Right now, she had to get out—she had to get back to her dad.

"Not today, Chimpanzombies!" June yelled as she flew toward the gates. "See ya later!"

She was laughing as she went through the exit, but when she passed the threshold, the forest didn't appear. There were no trees or hiking trails or overgrown bushes. Instead, she was somehow back in the park, right back at the carousel. She hadn't escaped at all.

"How did I get back here?" she asked, confused.

She was about to return to the exit when the Skyflinger appeared again. This time it was ready for her. It struck the fish with its giant mechanical arm, knocking June to the ground. She stumbled back, trying to find cover under the carousel and accidentally hitting a fish. It flew into the air.

It was just the distraction she needed. The Skyflinger went after it, trying to knock it away. June released another fish, and then three more, sending them soaring. The Skyflinger attacked each one, but it wasn't long before it was focused on her again. This time she had no escape route. The Skyflinger reached out for her, its giant arm just inches away.

"I got you, June!" a voice called out.

June looked up, spotting Greta charging

toward her. Greta had managed to get free of the swing, and now she grabbed on to one of the last carousel fish with her teeth. She ran around the carousel in a circle, tangling up the Skyflinger's mechanical arm, slowly bringing it to the ground.

June squeezed her eyes shut. She didn't dare move. Then she heard Greta's voice again, more urgent than before.

"Come with me!" Greta shouted. "Hurry!"

Chapter 12

It took them a while to get to the safe house, which was a water tower on the far edge of the park. As soon as they were all there, Greta started shouting orders. "Gus, Cooper, check the north and west perimeter wires," she said. "Steve, get to the lookout and make sure we weren't followed."

The three of them ran around, doing what they were told, and Greta secured the door to make sure no one could get inside. June's heart was still racing from earlier. She took a deep breath, trying to calm down.

"You're alive!" Boomer emerged from the other room. "I was so, so worried. I didn't know what to do. I started baking marshmallow calzones."

Greta didn't even smile. "We lost Happy Happy Land…."

"We did?" Boomer's brown eyes were sad.

"That's over half the park gone now," Greta said solemnly.

"What happens if we lose the other half?" Gus asked.

"Yeah, what's going to happen to us?" Cooper asked.

"I don't know," Gus muttered. "But at least we have calzones."

"And her." Boomer pointed at June.

"Her?" Greta sounded annoyed. "When the going got tough, she ran for the exits."

"I need to get home to my dad." June tried to defend herself.

Greta looked skeptical. "And if she really

did create Wonderland, whatever that means," she went on, "she would know that those exits aren't really exits anymore!"

"Well, they *were* exits when my mom and I created the park," June snapped back. "Sorry I wasn't around when this whole place went haywire, and it became impossible to exit from an exit marked EXIT."

Steve climbed down the ladder leading to the lookout and peeked into the room. "Did you know *exit* comes from the Latin verb *exeo-exitum*, which derives from the Greek verb *eximi-exite*?" June and Greta shot him annoyed looks. "Seems I backed into the middle of something here...."

For a minute, everyone was silent.

"Okay." Boomer tried to lighten the mood. "So we know the only way to open the exits is to get the park back up and running. Turning on Clockwork Swings is the key to that."

"There's no way to turn it back on," Cooper said.

"Yeah, we've been there a bunch of times," Gus added. "Looked at it every which way—"

"But she hasn't," Boomer said, pointing to June. "And if she created it, she can fix it."

"*Uhhhh...*" June murmured. This was starting to feel like a lot of pressure.

"So Wonderland is just a figment of your imagination?" Greta asked.

"Something like that," June said.

"Let me guess," Greta went on. "That means we're all figments of your imagination."

June tilted her head to the side, trying to decide how to answer that. How was she supposed to tell the mascots they existed only because of her? That they were tiny dolls she designed with her mom years ago? That they were only as real as she'd made them?

"I wouldn't put it exactly—"

"Oh, an existential crisis!" Steve laughed. "I knew this day was missing something!"

Greta looked skeptical. "Well, you can imagine this may be a little hard for us to wrap our heads around. Perhaps you will indulge me with some proof...."

"Fine!" June put her hands on her hips. If Greta wanted proof, she would give her a whole bunch of it. "Every morning, Steve drinks his morning tea: two point six grams of loose Earl Grey to two hundred and fifty milliliters of eighty-six-point-one-degree water, steeped for three minutes and eleven seconds and garnished to perfection with a spot of almond milk."

It was so quiet in the water tower June could hear each of her breaths. The beavers were nodding, recognizing every word

June said. One of Steve's quills popped out in embarrassment.

"Haha!" Boomer laughed. "See? All hail June!"

"Yeah, let's not get carried away," June said. "But I may be able to fix Clockwork Swings."

Greta snorted. "Look, these guys have suffered a lot already. And I'm willing to follow your lead here, 'cause I'm running out of options, but you gotta promise there's a real shot at this. Tell me that you're not serving up false hope."

June looked into Greta's warm brown eyes. Even now that they were away from the Chimpanzombies, Greta was still protecting her friends. She was a natural leader, and June respected that. She'd never lie to her.

"Well, I was pretty good at fixing things," June said. "But you gotta get me to Clockwork Swings."

Greta stared at June, and June stared right back. Then June snorted. A tiny, playful snort to show Greta she was serious. Greta snorted her reply.

June smiled.

She was pretty sure they'd reached an agreement.

Chapter
13

The group started through the park, keeping their eyes on their surroundings. June walked in the middle of the mascots, with Gus and Cooper flanking her on either side, and Greta and Boomer covering the front and the back. Steve was using the journey to ask June a million questions.

"Just walk me through this, would you?" he said, striding beside her. "I understand making Boomer the Welcome Bear of the park, and it makes proper sense that the beavers would be builders, but why did it seem like a good idea to make the quill-covered porcupine the safety officer?"

"I don't know!" June laughed. "I was six. My mom gave me a pincushion."

Steve did not seem to like that answer.

"I am nobody's pincushion, sister," he quipped.

"I came up with you around the same time I gave Gus the power to yodel in four languages," June explained.

"Little old lady, who!" Gus sang out. *"Viejita, quien! Petite vieille dame, qui! Kleine alte dame!"*

"Keep it down!" Cooper whispered. He put his paw over Gus's mouth. "The Chimpanzombies will hear us."

That was all it took for the two beavers to break into a huge argument. They got in each other's faces and started name-calling. Boomer shook his head disapprovingly. "Those two…"

"They shouldn't be fighting all the time," June agreed.

"Well, they never used to, but ever since that got here..." Boomer stared up at the Darkness. "Why did you create it, June?"

"I didn't, Boomer," she tried.

"But I thought you created everything in the park...."

June had thought so, too. But why would she create something so terrible? She never wanted anything bad to happen to the mascots. She loved them, even though she'd stopped playing with them as much as she used to.

"Come on, slowpokes!" Greta called out from the front. "The clocks are just up ahead!"

They climbed the hill toward Clockwork Swings. Greta stayed in front, making sure it was safe, while the beavers and Boomer fell behind. Steve spent the last part of the journey admiring Greta's beautiful reddish-brown coat, her boar strut, and her "come-hither" tusks. June laughed, realizing he was totally smitten with her.

"Oh boy," June said as she approached the Clockwork Swings tower. She stared at the control panel with all its buttons and wires. "This is a little more complicated than the model we made."

She climbed underneath the ride and stared at the open gears. "The hydraulics seem to be sealed and stuff," she called to the mascots. "No leaks or anything. It must be that one of the gears is jammed."

"Eureka!" Boomer cried. "She's fixing it! We're witnessing a miracle!"

"More of a diagnosis," Steve corrected. "But it does bring us closer to a solution."

June studied the gears, trying to figure out which one was causing the problem. She was used to taking things apart and putting them back together again. She'd fixed the vacuum and the toaster, but this was a little different. The ride was massive.

She pulled the blueprint out of her pocket, comparing the technical drawing to the actual gears.

"I gotta get this ride started," she said. "And I know you have the answer. Please tell me the answer...."

June held the blueprint up to the light. When her mom had drawn the heart, she'd covered a little bit of the Clockwork Swings model. It was difficult to see where the drawing and the real gears matched up.

"Well, what does it say?" Greta asked.

"I can't see. My name's covering it.... Ugh, Mom," she said under her breath. "Why did you write on this?"

June moved around, trying to get a better look at the gears. Everywhere she went, Greta trailed behind her, as if she were just waiting for June to admit she couldn't fix it.

"Don't do this to me," Greta said, frustrated. "It's your blueprint, isn't it?"

June turned back, worried the others were listening. Boomer had fallen asleep at some point. Thankfully, Steve and the beavers didn't seem to be paying too close attention.

"Yeah," June said. "But it's been a while since—"

Just then Boomer rolled over in his sleep and whacked Steve with his paw. Boomer shot straight up, feeling the quills go right through his skin. Steve was stuck to the giant bear. He started to panic and more quills shot out of him.

"Duck and cover!" Steve yelled as three more gray quills went flying.

"Look out!" Gus screamed.

But it was too late. One of the quills came at June and pierced the blueprint piece, sending it shooting through the air. Cooper reached for it but missed. Then

Gus took a running leap off Cooper's back and grabbed the quill as it passed.

"Got it!" Gus yelled.

He held up the quill in triumph. There was one problem: The blueprint wasn't on it anymore. It had ripped off and was now floating in the wind.

"We need that blueprint!" June cried, running after it.

Gus and Cooper joined her, trying as hard as they could to catch it. But every time they got close, it blew just a little farther out of reach. Greta and Boomer joined in the chase, too, running up toward Fireworks Falls, but as Boomer went, he accidentally knocked Steve into a trash bin. Steve was stuck in place. All the bits of garbage were now lodged in his quills.

"Stop!" Steve called out after them. "Fireworks Falls is a deathtrap!"

But June was running so fast she couldn't hear him.

Chapter 14

We have to get it!" June yelled, darting out onto the glass walkway that led to Fireworks Falls. "We can't lose it, guys!"

Gus and Cooper ran over to Boomer.

"Throw me—I'll get it!" Gus said, watching as the piece drifted farther away.

"No, throw *me*!" Cooper argued.

"No, no, throw *me*!" Gus said.

"Throw *both* of them!" June knew they had only a few seconds before their chance was gone. Boomer grabbed a beaver in each paw and sent them hurtling through the air. They were still fighting, whacking each other with their tails and yelling about who would get to it first. They landed on the observation deck with a thud, but the blueprint was already gone.

"Your fault," Cooper grumbled. He narrowed his green eyes at Gus.

June and the rest of the mascots caught up to them. Together they watched the blueprint drift farther away.

"You've got to be kidding me!" June said. "Of all the—"

"Enough!" a voice yelled.

They turned to see Steve, who was standing behind them. His gray quills were sticking up in every direction. He kicked a fast food container off his foot.

"I command you to remove yourself from this platform!" he said. "I have been putting up with this reckless abandon for months on end, and it is chipping away at my soul. I'm so very tired—what...what is that sound?"

Tink! Tink! Tink!

A faint creaking was coming from somewhere below them. June looked down, noticing that the glass walkway of the observation deck was now spider-webbed with cracks. Far below, a dozen Chimpanzombies in mountain-climbing gear were making their way up the glass walkway, clinging to it with ice axes.

"Oh no…" June whispered.

Seeing the group, the Chimpanzombies chipped away even faster.

"Fear not," Steve said. "We simply must reach higher ground!"

But when they looked up, toward the top of Fireworks Falls, they saw a dozen more Chimpanzombies. Wooden boards covered the mouth of the falls. The chimps were prying them off one by one.

The Chimpanzombies sped up, winding the machinery of the falls up to speed until the whole top of it blew off. All the fireworks started going off at the same time. There was nowhere to hide. A whole wall of explosives was raining down on them.

"Run!" Greta yelled.

She darted out in front, leading the group to a few lunch tables on the other side of the observation deck. Each one was covered with a large umbrella. They ran as fast as they could, but they couldn't get there in time. The fireworks smashed into the observation deck, breaking it into pieces.

June felt the ground beneath her feet slipping and then coming apart. She grabbed on to one of the tables and felt it tip to the side. All at once she was falling, falling...until she wasn't anymore. She looked down, realizing she was on the one section of deck that hadn't completely broken away.

"Hold on, June!" Greta called from

below. The mascots had made their way onto the nearby shore, using a giant railing as a slide to guide their fall. Now they were all staring up at her.

June clung to the table. She glanced up, noticing a Chimpanzombie right above her. It inched forward, a mischievous grin on its face. With one final *tink!* of its pickax, it broke the piece of glass that held the table in place. June plunged toward the river below.

Thinking quickly, Boomer tossed one of the broken umbrellas into the water, creating a little boat. It skimmed across the river's fiery surface and caught June just in time. She was safe, sailing downstream, the wind whipping through her hair. In that moment she felt fearless, untouchable. There was nothing the Chimpanzombies could do to stop her.

She spotted a waterfall ahead. She used all her body weight to pull back the umbrella, blocking the sparks that poured down onto the boat. She was completely sheltered from them, but her plan wasn't foolproof. Within seconds the umbrella started to disintegrate.

She didn't have long before she was in serious trouble. The makeshift boat was coming apart. She went around a quick turn and launched herself and her umbrella boat off a rock, landing in calm waters below.

"You're okay," she said, smiling. "You're okay, June. It's okay!"

But when the umbrella spun around, she spotted another huge drop ahead of her. In an instant, she went hurtling over the falls. She flew through the air, careening out over the park and landing on top of a giant statue of Boomer.

She sat there, catching her breath. It took a moment before she was truly sure she was safe. She'd somehow made it out of the falls. Her heart was pounding, but she was okay.

She stared into the distance. The mascots were watching her. They were so happy they were practically jumping up and down. She'd made it to shore.

"You did it!" Greta yelled.

"Well done!" Steve cheered.

June couldn't help smiling. Then she got up, brushed herself off, and ran to meet them by the ravine.

But when June got to the bridge that hung across the ravine, she discovered it was broken. Some of the Chimpanzombies had ruined that, too. The sun was setting, and there was no easy way to get back to her friends, so she decided to go through Slot Canyon to find them. It was already dark when she started her hike down.

"*Oh my,*" she sang as she trekked across the sand. "*Here comes pi. Three point one four—*"

Suddenly, the ground beneath her gave out. She dropped through a trapdoor in the bottom of the canyon. But her feet never hit the floor. Instead she floated out and up, completely weightless.

"Zero G Land!" she said, excited. She'd totally forgotten it was here.

June somersaulted through space, enjoying how good it felt to be free from gravity. This place was even more magical than she'd imagined it could be. She was tumbling and turning against the night sky when she spotted a village in the distance. There was a strange house covered with balloons. It floated out in front of the stars.

She'd designed Zero G Land with trampolines throughout it, so you could launch yourself from one place to the next, building momentum. Now June launched herself toward the house, aiming at the window. When she got there, she clung to the shutters and peered inside. Piles and piles of candy were spread out on the floor of the living room. A familiar figure hunched over them. He worked quickly, sorting them according to color.

"Peanut..." June said to herself. Then she knocked on the window to get his attention. "Hey, Peanut!"

Peanut stood, and then he disappeared from view. June peered inside but couldn't see him anymore. She wasn't quite sure what was happening when the window opened and she was yanked inside. Peanut slammed the shutters behind her.

"What are you doing?" he asked. "Are you crazy?"

June just ignored him. "You're alive!" she said. "I knew—"

"Who are you?" Peanut asked. He stared at her intensely.

"I'm June! I'm a friend of Greta and Boomer...actually, everyone." She couldn't believe she was here, with Peanut. All this time he'd been stuck in Zero G Land. He was safe. "They're gonna be so happy. Let's go find them!"

June reached out her hand, but Peanut pulled away.

"No, no, no..." he muttered.

"Come on," June said. "I lost them at Fireworks Falls."

"No," Peanut said firmly. "Maybe tomorrow or something. I'm very busy."

"Busy?" June repeated. "What could be more important than finding your friends?"

Peanut stared at her, his green eyes wide. He was exactly as cute and furry as the toy version of him. Just looking at him, she wanted to give him a huge hug.

"I'm not going out there, okay? I'm never going out there again," he said.

They stared at each other for a moment, and June finally understood. He was serious. He was afraid.

"I just can't, okay? I have work to do...."

Peanut settled back down next to the candy. "I gotta sort the candy."

June took a deep breath. This wasn't the joyful mascot she'd imagined years before. Peanut had been the life of the park, creating all its rides with his magic marker. Everyone loved him. Everyone looked up to him.

"Peanut..." June started. "What happened to you?"

He didn't look up from the piles of candy. "What do you mean, what happened to me? The Chimpanzombies had me, I was able to escape, and I made it up here. And now I'm sorting candy. It was a mess when I got here—believe me."

Peanut stopped, noticing something in one of the piles. He grabbed a stray piece of candy and stared at it, horrified.

"What—stripes?!" he said in disbelief. "If I'm not on every minute, there will be anarchy. Chaos."

"Look," June said, watching as Peanut dropped the candy into another pile. "If you're afraid of the park—"

"I'm not scared of the park," Peanut replied. "It's just…It's safe in here."

"But you're alone—"

"Where nothing can hurt me."

"Well, you can't stay in here forever," June tried.

"Says who?" Peanut asked. "There's no rules for something like this."

"Something like what?"

"To losing everything!" Peanut said, exasperated. "The world out there is just a reminder of all that's lost."

"But not everything's gone," June said. "Greta, Boomer…they're all still there."

"I can't bear to look them in the eye."

"Why?" June asked. "Do you think they blame you?"

"They don't blame me," Peanut said.

"They count on me. And I...I can't deliver. Not anymore."

"Sure you can. I know how this works. You just wave your marker—" June went to grab the marker, but Peanut stopped her.

"Put that back," he said softly.

"And you can make anything come true."

Peanut stared at June, his eyes sad. "I wish it still worked that way."

"But you're Peanut the Splendiferous!" June said, trying to cheer him up. "All these amazing things in Wonderland— they came from you."

"That is a lie," Peanut said finally. He hung his head, unable to look her in the eye.

"Huh?"

"I was just the middleman," Peanut admitted. "All the ideas, the inspiration, it came from..."

June took a deep breath, realizing what he meant. "A voice whispering in your ear," she said, finishing his sentence.

"How do you know about that?" Peanut asked. "I never told anyone."

"It doesn't matter."

"And not too long ago," Peanut continued, "the sound of her voice...it just..."

"Went away," they said together.

June nodded, understanding what had happened. After her mom got sick, June hadn't wanted to play with Wonderland anymore, and all the wonder she'd put into it had gone with her. She'd abandoned Peanut. He couldn't keep Wonderland going without her, not when there wasn't anyone telling him where to go and what to create. He didn't know what to make with his magic marker if he didn't hear her mom whispering the directions in his ear.

"And then the Darkness took over..." June said.

"I guess, whoever it was," Peanut said, "she forgot about me. I kept waiting. I kept hoping she would come back to help me fight against the Darkness. But I just felt so..."

"Alone."

The two stood together in the middle of the living room, feeling the sadness of the past months. Everything had fallen apart so quickly. June had never meant to let the light inside her go dark, but when her mom went away, everything was so hard. How was she supposed to keep shining, as her mom said, when she was so afraid all the time? How could she take care of Wonderland when she was worried about her dad?

She looked down at the marker in her hand. "Peanut," she started. "I need to tell you something...."

But just then Peanut sprang forward and pressed his finger against June's lips. "*Shhhhh!*" he said, his eyes wide.

Then June heard it, too—the sound of the Chimpanzombies in the distance. They were in Zero G Land, and they were coming toward the house.

"We have to go!" Peanut cried.

Then he reached out and grabbed June's hand.

Chapter
16

They ran up the stairs and into a small tower connected to the house. From the upper windows, June had a view of the whole floating city. A long line of Chimpan-zombies streamed through, bouncing off the different buildings and trampolines, getting closer.

"Every day, every day is a wonderful day, is a wonderful day in Wonderland!" they sang, their voices echoing across Zero G Land.

"They found us!" Peanut said. "They must've followed you in!"

The lead Wonder Chimp doll was dressed as a gym teacher, and he ordered the rest of the Chimpanzombies around. He blew his whistle several times, and the dolls launched themselves one by one up toward June and Peanut.

"We need to move—now," Peanut said.

He grabbed June's hand and jumped out of the tower, aiming for a large trampoline below. They floated downward and hit it, and then they ricocheted toward another trampoline farther off. But the impact was so strong the marker slipped from June's grasp. It floated out in space, just beyond her reach.

"Your marker!" June said, trying to figure out how they could get it back.

"Leave it," Peanut said. "It's worthless."

"No, it's not!" June said, launching herself toward it.

She was so focused that she didn't notice that the Chimpanzombies had spotted her and changed course, coming right at her.

"Look out, June!"

When June glanced up, the swarm of Chimpanzombies was moving in fast. Peanut launched himself through the air and began fending them off, trying to buy her more time. She flew toward the marker. It was heading to another trampoline, so she changed her trajectory to meet it after impact. As soon as it bounced off, she soared toward it and caught it in her hand.

She had it. She had Peanut's magic marker!

"Oh no!" June cried, unable to stop herself. There was nothing to catch hold of. Now she was on a collision course with a pack of Chimpanzombies.

"Gotcha!" a familiar voice said. Peanut grabbed her, and they were both floating in space, casting out on another course.

"There's no way out," June said, eyeing the exits. They were all blocked by the Chimpanzombies.

"There is for you," Peanut said. Before June understood what was happening, Peanut grabbed on to a lamppost they were floating past. He wound around it like a gymnast, still holding on to June and picking up speed. Just when they were spinning as fast as they could, he released her, sending her careening toward the edge of the floating village.

Once June landed at the exit, she turned back. The Chimpanzombies were descending on Peanut. They surrounded him in a giant swarm.

"June! Go!" he called out to her, waving her away.

She did what he said, but as she reached solid ground, she couldn't stop thinking about how Peanut had saved her. What would happen to him? Was this the last time she'd ever see him in Wonderland? How could the park go on without its genius creator?

June ran through the park, trying to make her way back to Fireworks Falls. Now that she had Peanut's magic marker, they could repair the park one ride at a time, but she'd need the mascots' help to do it. First, they had to save Peanut. He had to hold the magic marker for it to work. If they could only rescue him...if they could only get away from the Chimpanzombies long enough to use it....

She turned back, staring up at the Darkness that loomed in the sky. She'd created it, just as she'd created everything else in Wonderland. After her mother got sick, June couldn't bear to spend all day creating and designing the park, and without her love and attention, it had slowly fallen apart.

She'd never let her fear take over again. She couldn't let down the mascots; she couldn't let down Peanut.

She picked up speed, racing toward Fireworks Falls.

In that instant June just knew her mom would be okay, that the summer would pass, and then she'd come home. June's dad had said her treatments were working. She'd get better. And when she did, June wanted Wonderland to be as wondrous as it had always been when they were together. She wanted her own light to be brighter than it ever had been before. She knew exactly what she needed to do. She had the skills as a builder and an inventor to rebuild the park.

She was going to save Wonderland—before it was too late.

WONDER PARK

HUGGABLE BOOMER PLUSH

SCENTED WONDER CHIMP PLUSH

FLYING FISH CAROUSEL

BUILD YOUR OWN WONDER CHIMP

FIGURES

Over 1,400 Combinations!

Funris